Annie Wilkins and the Mystery at Stone Mountain

Anna Maria Sands

High Noon Books
Novato, California

Cover Design and Illustrations: Tina Cash

International Standard Book Number: 0-87879-576-6

5 4 3 2 1 0 9 8 7 6
2 1 0 9 8 7 6 5 4 3

You'll enjoy all the High Noon Books.
Write for a free full list of titles.

Contents

CHAPTER ONE

A Good Day for a Hike

It was early in the morning. The noise that Lucky, her pigeon, was making woke her up.

Annie sat up. It was still dark. "Lucky, what's the matter?" she asked.

Lucky kept on walking around in his cage.

Annie got out of bed and walked over to Lucky's cage. "OK,OK. Take it easy," she said.

She turned on the lamp next to the cage

"Here's come corn. Now be quiet," she said.

Then she saw the note tied to Lucky's leg.

1

This is what it said,

Hi Annie,
How about a
hike up to Moss
beach tomorrow?
Call me. Sally

Annie thought to herself, "Here it is, Saturday. I wanted to sleep in. Now I'm wide awake. And it's only 4:30." She turned out the light and went back to bed.

When she woke up again at 8:30, she went right to the phone. "I better call Sally before she calls me," she said.

Sally answered the phone. "You got my note," Sally said.

"I sure did. Lucky woke me up at 4:30. What's all this about a hike to Moss Beach?" Annie asked.

"Well, I saw Ham and Bugs last night. Terry and I went to Pete's Ice Cream store last night. We both had a milk shake. Ham said that he and Bugs were going to hike up to Stone Mountain. I thought we could all meet there," Sally asked.

Annie liked Ham. What a great way to spend a Saturday. "What are they going to do at Stone Mountain?" Annie asked.

"Bugs wants to find a bee nest up there. He thinks he can get the honey," Sally said.

"I thought no one lives up near the top," Annie said.

"Well, they used to use the old tower as a lookout for fires. It's still there. But they built a new one over at Loop Mountain. That's why Bugs thinks there could be some nests up there at Stone Mountain. That old tower has been empty so long," Sally said.

"And Moss Beach, up at the lake, is close to Stone Mountain," Annie said.

"You're right. We can pack a lunch and share it with Ham and Bugs. What do you think?" Sally asked.

"I love it. Sally, you're a peach. I'll be at your house in thirty minutes with the sandwiches," Annie said.

"Right on," Sally answered.

Annie quickly got dressed. Then she rushed into the kitchen. She started to make ten sanwiches. Just then her mother, Mrs. Wilkins, walked in. "Annie, what are you doing?"

"Sally, Terry, and I are going to take a hike to Moss Beach up at the lake. We're going to meet Ham and Bugs. We're all fixing lunch," Annie said.

"Well, let me help. I'll finish the sandwiches. Get the picnic basket," Mrs. Wilkins said.

"Mom, you're swell!" Annie said.

By the time the basket was filled, Annie had her hiking clothes on. "It's going to be warm today. How are you getting up to the lake?" Mrs. Wilkins asked

"We're going to ride our bikes to the front of the park. We'll leave them there and hike in," Annie said.

"Well, take care. And don't be home too late. I don't want any of you running around when it's dark," Mrs. Wilkins said.

"Don't worry. We'll be careful," Annie said. Then she grabbed the picnic basket and went to her bike.

"This is going to be fun," Annie said to herself. She tied the basket on to her bike. Then she was on her way to meet Terry at Sally's house.

As Annie was on her way to Sally's house, she was thinking about Ham and Bugs.

She was thinking about all the things they would do at Moss Beach. But she was thinking a little more about Ham.

Annie was glad that Sally thought of meeting Ham and Bugs up at the lake. Now that, she thought, was a great idea! She would have lots of time to talk with Ham!

CHAPTER TWO

Off for the Lake

Annie got to Sally's house just as Terry rode up.

Annie saw that Terry also had a picnic basket.

"I brought sandwiches. What did you bring?"
Annie asked.

"I brought soft drinks," Terry said.

Just then Sally walked out on the porch.
"Well, it seems we're all ready to get to the park."
She also had a picnic basket.

"I have sandwiches and Terry has the drinks.
What did you bring?" Annie asked.

"You know Ham and Bugs. They both like potato chips and fruit. So that's what I brought," Sally said.

"I think we have plenty of food," Annie said.

"This is going to be fun," Terry said.

Mrs. Washington, Sally's mother, walked out on the front porch. "Now you girls take care. Don't come back too late," she said.

"Mrs Washington, that's just what my mother told me," Annie said.

"See you all later," Mrs. Washington said.

The three girls got on their bikes, waved good-bye to Mrs. Washington, and started off for the park.

After thirty minutes Sally shouted, "Let's stop and rest. We're going to be going up hill starting here."

As they were sitting and talking,
two police cars drove by.

"A good idea," Terry called back.

The girls all stopped and got off their bikes. They sat down under some elm trees and leaned against them.

As they were sitting and talking, two police cars drove by.

"I'll bet they are looking for the robbers," Sally said.

"What robbers?" Annie asked.

"Didn't you hear what happened?" Sally asked.

"No. What's going on?" Annie asked.

"I heard it on the music radio station this morning," Sally said.

"What happened?" Annie asked.

"The Diamond Store was robbed last night. the police think there were two men who broke in," Sally said.

"Did they get very much?" Annie asked.

"Yes, they got plenty. Lots of rings and things," Sally said.

"What would robbers do with all those diamonds?" Terry asked.

"The police know what was taken. They think the robbers will have to hide the diamonds for a while. Then they'll sell it all a little at a time," Sally said.

"Well, shall we start off again?" Annie asked. She wanted to get up to Moss Beach right away. What a great day it would be!

"Annie, I think you want to meet Ham for lunch," Terry said.

"I sure do," Annie answered.

"Then off we go," Sally said.

Then they all got on their bikes and started up the long hill that went right to the park.

The last few miles the girls had to go were not easy. It was a steep climb up a twisting road. But they finally got to a big parking lot.

"Well, what do you know. We made it," Terry said.

"I'm tired," Sally said.

"Me, too. But I want to get to the beach. Let's park our bikes here and hike in. Come on. Let's get going," Annie said.

The girls got off their bikes and locked them. Then they got their picnic baskets and started walking up to the lake.

"Not another hill to go up," Terry said as she looked at the path.

"Don't worry, Terry. The lake isn't far. Anyway, it will be good for us," Annie said.

Sally laughed. "Very funny," she said.

Just over the top of a small hill, the girls saw the lake. "Look, there it is. Isn't it pretty?" Annie asked.

Sally pointed. "And just down there is Moss Beach."

"At last. Now we can go down hill," Annie said.

At the beach, the girls sat down. The sand was warm.

"You know what? It was worth it," Terry said.

"How right you are. what a pretty place," Annie said.

"And there's the tower," Sally said.

The girls looked across the lake. There were trees everywhere. But they could see the old tower at the top of Stone Mountain.

"I wonder if Ham and Bugs are at the top of it," Terry said.

"They could be. You know Bugs. He carries mirrors and all kinds of things with him when he's looking for bees," Annie said.

"Maybe they're even looking at us right now," Sally said.

"Could be," Annie said.

"Come on. Let's get the food under a tree. That will keep it cool," Sally said.

"And let's keep it all away from the ants," Terry said.

"That's a good idea," Annie said.

Then Terry called out. "Come on. Someone help me carry all this food." Terry saw a small tree near the beach. "Let's move everything over there."

Sally and Annie grabbed all their picnic baskets and carried them over to the tree. It was cool there.

"Well, the shades should help keep everything cool for a while," Annie said.

"Let's hope so. We sure don't want everything hot by the time Ham and Bugs get here." Sally said.

"How right you are," Annie said.

CHAPTER THREE

Two Strangers

Annie, Sally, and Terry knew that Ham and Bugs would not get to Moss Beach unitl noon. There were about ten other people sitting around the beach. Since it was only eleven o'clock, they all started to walk around and look at the moss and the lake.

All of a sudden they heard a horn honking. Then they saw a small truck near the lake. Two men were in the truck. One of them called out to the girls, "Hey, can you help us?"

The girls walked over near the truck. They looked at the two men. "What do you need?" Sally asked.

Bud and I are trying to get up to Stone Mountain
Do you know the way?

The man with the beard said, "Bud and I are trying to get up to Stone Mountain. Do you know the way?"

The girls looked at one another. "I know there is an old dirt road that goes up to the top. The rangers used to use it before they closed the old tower," Annie said.

"You mean the tower is closed?" Bud asked.

"Oh, yes. It's been closed for years. They built a new one up on Loop Mountain across the lake," Annie said.

"Do you think this road goes up to the old tower?" Lefty, the other man, asked.

"It might. Why do you want to go up there? No one has been there in years," Sally said.

"We're new to this town. We just want to get to know all the places a little better," Bud said.

"Yeah, we might move to your town for a while," Lefty said.

"Sorry we can't be of more help," Annie said.

"Thanks anyway," Bud said. Then the two men drove off.

Annie turned to Sally and Terry. "Those two guys gave me the creeps. I just didn't like them."

"Why?" Terry asked.

"I don't know. Just a feeling, I guess," Annie said.

"I didn't think they were so bad," Sally said.

"Well, why would anyone want to drive up to an old tower? If they are going to move to town, what are they doing up here at the lake?" Annie asked.

"Oh, well. Maybe they just like to drive around," Terry said.

"Come on. Let's get back to the beach. Maybe Ham and Bugs are on their way," Annie said.

"They better be. I'm getting hungry," Terry said.

The girls walked back to the beach and sat down. It was a good day. It was not real hot. It was nice. There was a little breeze. They all felt great.

Sally looked at her watch. "Where are those guys? It's 12:30. They should have been here by now."

"You know Bugs. If he found a bee nest, he's forgotten to look at his watch," Annie said.

"But Ham isn't that way," Terry said.

Just then, the girls heard someone calling, "Annie! Sally! Terry!"

"Look. I see someone down the beach. Could it be Bugs and Ham?" Sally asked.

"No. It's just one person," Annie said.

Sally shouted, "Ham! Bugs! We're over here."

The three girls started to wave. They were all shouting.

"That's Bugs. But where is Ham?" Annie yelled as Bugs got closer.

Bugs finally got to them and sat down. He was tired from running.

"Bugs, rest for a minute.
Where's Ham?" Sally asked.

24

"Bugs, rest for a minute. Where's Ham?" Sally asked.

Bugs did not say anything. He just sat for a minute. Then he said, "Ham and I were near the old tower. I wondered if there might be a bee nest near the top," Bugs said. Then he stopped.

"Yes, go on," Annie said.

"And where is Ham?" Terry asked.

"That's what I'm trying to tell you. Ham stayed down, just looking around. I took all my stuff to the top. Then Ham climbed up. He said he had seen an old blue truck with two men in it. Ham thought we should get off the tower," Bugs said.

"An old blue truck?" Terry asked.

"Were there two men in it? Did one of them have a beard?" Annie asked.

"I think so," Bugs said.

"Then what happened?" Annie asked.

"I left my stuff with Ham. He stayed up there to look for the truck and the men. He said he could see all of you from the tower. I climbed down to look around. Then I saw the two men climb up the tower. One of them had a small sack. I waited for Ham to come down. One man came down but he went back again. When the two men came down, I felt that something had happened to Ham," Bugs said.

"This doesn't make any sense to me," Sally said.

"I have a feeling that something has happened to Ham. Come on. Let's all get to the tower," Annie said.

Bugs looked up to the old tower. "Look. I see a light flashing from the tower. It must be Ham. Maybe he is using one of my mirrors. Maybe he is trying to tell us something!"

"Tell us what?" Annie asked.

"I don't know. I just have a feeling that something has gone wrong," Bugs said.

"Oh, Bugs. Let's hope not," Terry said.

Sally looked at Annie. "You sure looked worried."

"She can't be any more worried than I am," Terry said.

They all looked at one another. What should they do to find out what had happened to Ham?

Was he safe? Did he need help? What could all of them do?

CHAPTER FOUR

Back to the Tower

Annie looked at Bugs, Sally, and Terry. She knew something was wrong. She knew they all had to find out what happened to Ham.

"What do we do?" Terry asked.

"We can't just sit here and wait for Ham. We have to get up to the old tower to see if he is there," Annie said.

"What if he isn't?" Bugs asked.

"Let's take this one step at a time," Annie said.

"I agree with Annie. First, let's all get up there. If he isn't there, then we can take the next step," Sally said.

"What is the next step?" Terry asked.

"I don't know," Sally said.

"Bugs, how do you feel? Are you very tired? Can you make it back to the tower?" Annie asked.

"You bet I can. Come on," Bugs said.

They all got up and started walking up the hill and around the lake, to the old tower.

"How long did it take you to get to Moss Beach?" Annie asked Bugs.

"I think it took about thirty minutes," Bugs answered.

"Well, maybe if we all walk fast or run part of the way, we can get there sooner," Annie said.

As they were running along the old dirt road, Annie asked, "What were those two men doing up at the tower?"

"Remember, they said they wanted to take a look at the park. They said they were going to move to town," Sally answered.

"Well, this is really strange to me," Annie said.

It was not too long before Bugs stopped and said, "Well, there it is. Do you all see it?"

Above the trees, they could all see the ol tower.

"Now what do we do?" Annie asked.

31

"The three of you wait here. Let me climb up and see if Ham is up there," Bugs said.

"Shouldn't we look around to see if that blue truck is anywhere near here?" Annie asked.

"That's a good idea. Maybe those two men came back and parked off the road," Bugs said.

"Terry, you come with me. Annie and Sally, you two look around together. We'll all meet back here in fifteen minutes," Bugs said.

Bugs and Terry went one way. Annie and Sally went the other way. There was no sign of the blue truck anywhere near the tower.

When they all met again, Bugs said, "OK. I'm going to start climbing up the tower. I'll call down if I find Ham."

Bugs started off for the tower. Then he started to climb up.

As he was climbing, he looked back across the lake. He could see Moss Beach. He could see people sitting on the beach. They looked very small.

At the top of the tower, he slowly opened the door.

The first thing he saw was a small sack in the corner. Then he saw his pack with all of his things.

Then he saw Ham sitting in a chair. He was tied up. There was a gag over his mouth!

"Good grief! What's going on?" Bugs yelled.

He pulled a small knife from his pack. He cut the ropes that held Ham tied to the chair. Then he pulled the gag from Ham's mouth.

Then he saw Ham tied up in a chair.
There was a gag over his mouth.

"What happened?" Bugs asked.

"Let's get out of here," Ham said.

"Annie, Sally, and Terry are near the bottom of the tower. Let's get going. You can tell all of us what happened when we get down," Bugs said.

Bugs grabbed his stuff. Ham grabbed the small sack. Then they both started to the bottom of the tower.

When Annie saw Ham, she yelled, "Ham, what happened?"

"You'll never believe me," Ham said.

"Come on. Let's all get back to Moss Beach," Annie said.

Just then Bugs stopped. "Wait a minute. I have something to do," he said.

"Can't it wait?" Ham asked.

"No. But it won't take long. Start back for Moss Beach. I'll catch up with you in a few minutes," Bugs said. Then he left.

Annie, Ham, Sally, and Terry started on their way back.

As they were walking along, Annie said, "Ham, come on. We all need to know what happened."

Ham turned to her, "Annie, I better wait for Bugs to be with us. I have only part of the story."

"Part of the story?" Terry asked.

"That's right. It won't make any sense without Bugs telling his part," Ham answered.

"Well, maybe you're right. Maybe we should wait," Annie said.

Just then Sally said, "Look! Here comes Bugs. Now we can get the whole story."

Ham looked at Annie. "Do you think you can wait?" he asked.

"I think I can," Annie smiled.

"Great," Ham said as he winked at her.

CHAPTER FIVE

Ham Tells His Story

It was not long before all of them were back at Moss Beach. They all sat on the beach.

The girls brought the sandwiches and food out. Ham picked up a sandwich and bit into it.

"All right, Ham. Now tell us what happened after Bugs left the tower," Annie said.

"Before I say anything, let's look and see what's in that small sack," Ham said.

Bugs lifted the bag and reached in. "My gosh. It's glass, lots of pieces of glass," he said.

"Let me see." Annie reached in and pulled out a handful of diamonds and rings. "Bugs, I don't think these are glass. I think they are diamonds!"

*"Let me see." Annie reached in and pulled
out a handful of diamonds and rings.*

"Diamonds?" Bugs asked.

"Annie, those could be from that robbery at the Diamond Store last night," Sally said.

"They sure could be," Annie said.

"What could those diamonds be doing in that sack up here at Moss Beach?" Terry asked.

"I wonder if those two men had anything to do with the robbery," Annie asked.

"OK, Ham. Now, tell us what happened," Sally said.

Ham took another bite out of his sandwich. "When Bugs left me in the old tower, those two men came in. They had a small sack. One of them, the one with the beard, said he had to go to the truck for a minute."

"Then what happened?" Annie asked.

"The man who stayed up looked around the top of the tower. I knew something was wrong. That's when I got the mirror from Bugs' stuff. I tried to signal to all of you," Ham said.

"We saw the light. We didn't know what it meant," Sally said.

Go on, Ham," Terry said.

"The two men tied me up. They left the sack in the tower. They said they'd be back. I kept on hoping that Bugs would come back after they left," Ham said.

Annie handed Ham a Coke. "Thanks, Annie," Ham said. He winked at her.

Annie smiled back.

"Now what do we do?" Bugs asked.

"I think that all of us should take that sack to the police," Ham said.

"You're right, Ham. We'd better get it to them right away," Annie said.

The girls started to clean up the beach where they had all eaten. Ham stuck the small sack in with Bugs' bag of things. Then they all started back for the front of the park where their bikes were.

"I sure hope the police will be able to find those guys," Ham said.

"I don't think they'll have much trouble," Bugs said.

"How's that?" Annie asked.

Well, I wrote down the license number of the truck when I left Ham in the tower. I have it right here," Bugs said.

"And we all know what they look like," Sally said.

"Well, there's one more thing," Bugs said.

"What's that?" Annie asked.

"Before all of us left the tower to get back here, I did something that wasn't very nice," Bugs said.

They all stopped and looked at Bugs. "What was that?" Ham asked.

"You know that bee nest I was looking for?" Bugs asked.

"Yes," Ham answered.

"Well, I carefully carried it up into the tower," Bugs said.

"Bugs, you didn't," Annie said.

"Yes, I sure did. Those guys are going to have a few surprises when they come looking for Ham and the sack of diamonds, Bugs said.